MARTIN THE CAVEBINE

WRITTEN BY
SARA NICKERSON

ILLUSTRATED BY
DON WELLER

PUBLISHED BY
COMPREHENSIVE
HEALTH EDUCATION
FOUNDATION

22323 Pacific Highway South
Seattle, Washington 98198-7253

Library of Congress Card Number:
88-71369

ISBN 0-935529-06-3

Printed in the United States of
America.

MARTIN
THE
CAVEBINE

Deep in the Kivu forest, deeper than most
people go, there was a cave. It was a small
cave with a little stream running through the
middle. On the walls grew round wickerbarbs. Wickerbarbs gave off light, and made
the inside of the cave warm and cozy.

1

A happy group of cavebines lived in that cave in the Kivu forest. If you peeked quietly inside you would see them working, their small furry bodies moving quickly in the wickerbarb light. You would see them laugh and sing as they gathered food and swept the floor and polished the wickerbarbs so the cave wouldn't grow dark.

4

But you would have had to be very quiet if you wanted to see them, because cavebines were shy, timid creatures. They never left their cozy little cave and were very much afraid of the brightly lit forest. Well, almost all of them were afraid. All, except Martin.

Martin would sit at the front of the cave every day and stare out into the forest. "Martin," the other cavebines said as they gathered food from the side of the stream, "why don't you help us gather food for dinner?"

"I'm very busy right now," he answered. "I'm watching the animals who live in the forest. I'm learning how they gather food."

And when the cavebines picked up their brooms and cloths to sweep the cave floor and polish the wickerbarb lights, Martin didn't move from his place at the front of the cave.

"Why don't you help us, Martin?" they asked him again.

"I'm busy learning about the forest," he replied. "I'm watching the animals who live there. I'm learning where they go for shelter when it rains."

And once, when they were all gathered together to sing, Martin sat very still at the front of the cave. "What's the matter, Martin?" they asked him. "Don't you want to sing with us?"

"No, not right now," he whispered back. "There is danger in the forest today. I'm learning which are the best trees to climb for safety when there is danger."

"Martin," they said with hurt feelings, "you are a very different cavebine."

"I know," he said. "I know."

Day followed day and the cavebines lived happily in their home. Then one morning a strange thing happened. The wickerbarb lights which had always shone so brightly, began to grow dim. The cavebines polished and polished but it was no use—the wickerbarb lights grew fainter and fainter until suddenly, the cavebines were in total darkness. And, oh, were they scared!

11

"What shall we do?" they whispered to each other in the dark. "How will we live? How will we find food? How will we know who we're talking to?" Some of them started to cry.

"Don't worry," a strong voice said in the dark. "I think that maybe I can help this time."

"Martin?" they asked. "Is that you?"

"Yes," he said. "Now follow these directions."

14

Martin gathered all the cavebines together and told them to hold hands. When everyone was ready, he slowly led them to the tiny opening at the front of the cave.

"**F**ollow me," he said as he squeezed through the opening and into the bright, sunlit forest. Slowly, the other cavebines crawled through the hole and stepped timidly into the forest. They blinked their eyes many times to get used to the sunshine.

"Here," said Martin skipping over to a small bush. "These berries are good to eat." He picked a handful and brought it over to the other cavebines still huddled together in a circle. "Try them, they're very good," he said.

One by one, the other cavebines reached out their hands and took the berries. Slowly, they put them into their mouths. "Hey!" they said, "these are good. Very good! What else can we eat, Martin?"

Martin showed them which berries were good to eat and which were not. He showed them how to dig deep into the ground for roots. He showed them where to go for cover when it rained and which trees were good to climb for protection when danger was near. He showed them how to live in the forest and be friends with the animals who lived there.

23

That night, they huddled together sleepily at the grassy foot of a large oak tree, listening to the strange night noises that a forest makes.

"The forest is a different place, but a very good place for a cavebine to live," said one of the cavebines.

"Yes," said Martin. "Yes it is."

"And you are a different cavebine, but a very special cavebine, Martin," said another.

"Yes, I know," said Martin. "Thank you."

"No. Thank *you*," said the other cavebines
as they fell asleep in the deep, warm grass,
surrounded by the soft glow of many stars.

The end.

Other Health Education Titles Available from CHEF®

Becoming Male and Female
by Evelyn E. Ames and Lucille Trucano
• a book which helps young adults understand and accept their sexuality as a healthy, normal part of who they are
• recommended for young adults and health education teachers

Face to Face
by Neal Starkman
• the story of a teenage boy and girl's decision about whether or not to have sex, and how they independently conclude that abstinence is the best choice for them
• recommended for young adults
• included in the AIDS curriculum, *Here's Looking At AIDS And You*™

Martin the Cavebine
by Sara Nickerson
• a story which provides children with an understanding and appreciation of how people are unique and worthy of consideration
• recommended for children
• included in the drug education curriculum, *Here's Looking At You, 2000*®

The Roller Coaster: A Story of Alcoholism and the Family
by Don Fitzmahan
• a story which helps children in alcoholic families learn about their feelings and how to express them
• recommended for children
• included in the drug education curriculum, *Here's Looking At You, 2000*®

Miraculous Me
by Carl Nickerson, Cheryl Lollis, and Elaine Porter
• a book devoted to building the self-esteem of children
• recommended for adults

Peter Parrot, Private Eye
by Sara Nickerson
• the story about a parrot who finds out about how people use alcohol
• recommended for children
• included in the drug education curriculum, *Here's Looking At You, 2000*®

Preparing for the Drug (Free) Years: A Family Activity Book
• a book which provides families with information and practical skills to help prevent their children from getting involved with drugs
• recommended for parents of children in grades 4 through 7

Your Decision
by Neal Starkman
• a book which lets the reader make decisions about relationships, drugs, and sex, select any of dozens of paths based on those decisions; and explore the consequences of those decisions
• recommended for young adults
• included in the AIDS curriculum, *Here's Looking at AIDS and You*™

Z's Gift
by Neal Starkman
• the story of how a young boy responds to the news that his teacher has AIDS, and how he teaches adults the meaning of compassion
• recommended for children
• included in the AIDS curriculum, *Here's Looking at AIDS And You*™

To order or to get more information:
CHEF®
22323 Pacific Highway South
Seattle, Washington 98198-7253
206/824-2907